HER WORST NIGHTMARE . . .

Annie and Jake watched in horror as the rock at the mouth of the cave teetered, settled back, and then teetered again. Suddenly it came loose, tumbling down and landing at their feet.

"Look out!" shrieked Annie. She jumped aside, pulling Jake after her. Trouble scampered away into the underbrush.

The rocks tumbled and smashed and crashed against one another, raising a cloud of dust.

Finally, when all was still and the dust was settling, Annie dared to look at the cave opening. Her worst nightmare had come true. The entrance was completely clear, and standing just inside was Frankenturkey!

Read these other BONE CHILLERS **from HarperPaperbacks:**

*coming soon

BONE CHILLERS

FRANKENTURKEY II

BETSY HAYNES

HarperPaperbacks

A Division of HarperCollins*Publishers*

HarperPaperbacks *A Division of* HarperCollins*Publishers*
10 East 53rd Street, New York, N.Y. 10022

Copyright © 1995 by Betsy Haynes and Daniel Weiss Associates, Inc.

Cover art copyright © 1995 Daniel Weiss Associates, Inc.

All rights reserved. No part of this book may be used or reproduced in any manner whatsoever without written permission of the publisher, except in the case of brief quotations embodied in critical articles and reviews. For information address Daniel Weiss Associates, Inc., 33 West 17th Street, New York, New York 10011.

First printing: November 1995

Printed in the United States of America

HarperPaperbacks and colophon are trademarks of HarperCollins*Publishers*

❖10 9 8 7 6 5 4 3

For my friend, Samuel Mark Moldovan, of Monroeville, PA.

FRANKENTURKEY II

Chapter

Annie Duggan gazed forlornly out the family-room window as she twisted a lock of her brown hair between her fingers. The backyard of their old Massachusetts farmhouse was filled with gloomy afternoon shadows. A cold November wind whistled against the shuddering windowpane and Annie shivered. She noticed that snow had begun to pile up in the empty turkey pen beside the garage.

"Oh, Gobble-de-gook, I miss you so much," Annie whispered. "Why did you have to leave me?" It had been almost six months since her pet turkey had died.

"Who are you talking to?" her brother Kyle

asked, munching a chocolate chip cookie as he came in from the kitchen. He looked around the empty room and shrugged. Kyle was older and bigger than Annie, and thought he knew everything.

Annie lowered her eyes. "Nobody," she said.

"Yes, you were. I heard you," Kyle insisted.

Annie sighed. "I was just talking to Gobble-de-gook. Why did he have to die, anyway?"

Last year, when her parents had bought the bird to raise for Thanksgiving dinner, both Annie and Kyle had instantly loved him. They had cared for him together, and saved him from becoming the family's holiday meal.

But Kyle didn't seem to miss their pet at all.

"He was a stupid turkey," Kyle said in a superior tone. "He got out of his pen and ran in front of a truck. He didn't even know any better."

Annie glared at her brother. "How dare you call Gobble-de-gook stupid? I loved him, whether you did or not!" She hated when he used the word "stupid." Sometimes he acted as if it was the only word he knew.

"I loved him as much as you did and you

know it," Kyle fired back. "But turkeys do dumb stuff like that. Remember what Mr. Berkowitz at the feed store said?"

"Okay, you two. That's enough fighting."

Their mother came into the room and sat down at the big oak table in the corner to grade papers. She taught sixth grade at Winston Middle School, the same school Annie and Kyle attended.

"We weren't fighting," Kyle protested. "We were just having a discussion"—Kyle paused and grinned wickedly at his sister—"about how *stupid* Gobble-de-gook was to walk out in front of a truck. He must have learned that from Annie."

"Mo-*om!*" Annie shrieked.

But Mrs. Duggan pretended not to hear. "I have a project for the two of you. It will keep you too busy to fight. I want you to clean out the toy box." She nodded to an overflowing wooden box in the opposite corner. "It's so full the lid won't close."

"Oh, Mom, do we have to do it *now*?" Annie asked with a groan.

"Yeah, it's just full of junk," said Kyle. "We don't play with any of that stuff anymore."

"Exactly!" Mrs. Duggan said triumphantly.

"Thanksgiving is only a couple of weeks away, and Christmas will be here before you know it. I want it cleaned out so we can give away what you don't want and make room for new Christmas toys."

"Come on, Kyle. Let's get started," Annie said. She could tell from her mother's tone of voice that there was no use arguing and Kyle knew it, too.

Annie found things in the box she hadn't seen for months—games with pieces missing, her knee pads for her in-line skates, a fashion doll whose hair had fallen out, Kyle's catcher's mitt, and tons of just plain junk.

"Man, I'd forgotten all about this," exclaimed Kyle. "Look! It's the wishbone from"—he gulped and stared at the bone in his hand—"from *Frankenturkey!*"

Annie looked in horror at the huge bone.

"I'm glad we won't have to worry about him this year," she whispered.

"Me, too," Kyle whispered back.

Annie's mind raced backward to exactly one year ago.

"Remember how we tried to save Gobble-de-gook from becoming Thanksgiving dinner last year?" she asked.

4

Kyle nodded. "Yeah, we hid him in the woods and bought a frozen turkey at the supermarket to put in his pen and fake out Mom and Dad." Kyle grinned at the memory. "Remember how we hid in the garage to work on our bogus bird and how we used coat hangers to attach a Halloween mask for its head?"

"Of course I remember," said Annie. "And we were gluing feathers from my bed pillow onto his body when that storm came up and that bolt of lightning crashed through the window and zapped him into life, just like in the old Frankenstein story."

Annie and Kyle looked at each other solemnly and said in unison, *"Frankenturkey!"*

The huge monster bird had terrorized them, stalking and attacking them in a cave deep in the woods. But Annie and Kyle had gotten revenge. In fact, it was Frankenturkey they had eaten for Thanksgiving dinner!

They were still staring at the wishbone when their father came into the family room, the evening paper tucked under his arm.

"Well, look what you two turned up," he said, and chuckled. "The wishbone from last year's Thanksgiving dinner. I thought you were going to follow the old tradition of breaking it and making a wish."

"Um . . . we don't believe in that stuff," Kyle mumbled.

He's scared, Annie realized. *Does he really think the wishbone could make something bad happen?*

"You never know," Mr. Duggan said. "When I was a boy we used to fight over which two kids would get to break the wishbone. The wish came true for whoever got the biggest piece."

"Did you ever get the biggest piece and have your wish come true?" Annie asked.

A twinkle lit Mr. Duggan's eyes. "Of course. There's magic in wishbones."

Annie glanced at the bone again.

"Who knows?" Mr. Duggan said. "That old turkey bone may still be full of magic."

The big forked bone looked pretty harmless. Besides, they had been safe from Frankenturkey for almost a year, Annie reminded herself. He couldn't come back to hurt them because he was dead and they had eaten him.

"Do you think we should try it, Kyle?" she asked a little while later, when both their parents had left the room. "It might be fun."

6

"Try what?" Kyle asked. He was hunched over the toy box inspecting a basketball that was flat on one side.

"The wishbone," Annie said impatiently.

Kyle made a face. "Don't be stupid. Dad was just kidding."

Annie bristled. Lately, all Kyle did was put her down.

"Do you think Dad's stupid, too?" she challenged. "It was his idea."

Kyle gave her an annoyed look. "Okay, okay. If it will get you off my back." He reached for the bone and hesitated.

"What's the matter? Scared?" Annie taunted.

Kyle scowled at her and picked up the bone by one end. "Here, grab the other end and make a wish."

Annie smiled to herself. She knew exactly what she wanted to wish for.

"I wish Gobble-de-gook would come back to life and be our pet again," she said softly.

Kyle rolled his eyes. "Talk about stupid, that's the stupidest wish I ever heard," he muttered. "I wish my friend Jake Wilbanks would come over so that I could have somebody *smart* to talk to."

Annie pulled at her side of the bone. Kyle was pulling, too, but the bone didn't seem to want to break.

"It's so old it's probably petrified," grumbled Kyle.

"Come on. Try harder," Annie urged.

This time she used both hands and pulled as hard as she could. The bone bent.

SNAP!

"It broke! It broke!" Annie cried, hopping up and down and holding her piece up in the air. "I got the biggest piece! My wish comes true!"

"No, you didn't," said Kyle. "I did. See?" He stuck his piece of the bone under her nose. "If you don't believe me, let's measure." Annie held out her piece, and they touched them together.

"Oh, no," said Kyle. "One piece is supposed to be bigger than the other, but they're both the same size. We broke the wishbone exactly in half."

"But . . ." Annie looked down at the two halves of the giant wishbone. They *were* exactly the same size. The top part where the sides connected had split right down the middle. "Does that mean neither of our wishes will come true?" she asked sadly.

Suddenly Trouble, the Duggans' big golden retriever, got up off the cushion where he'd been napping. A deep growl rumbled in the back of his throat. Running to the door, he raised up on his hind legs and started barking like crazy.

The doorbell rang.

"Down, Trouble. Down, boy," Kyle called as he rushed to answer the door.

Jake Wilbanks was standing on the front step, snow frosting his down jacket and knitted cap.

Kyle's wish had just come true.

Chapter

Annie stomped up the stairs to her room, leaving the boys laughing and talking together in front of the fire. It wasn't fair! She knew it was probably just a coincidence that Jake happened to come over at exactly the same moment Kyle made his wish. But that didn't matter. Kyle would drive her crazy for the next month teasing her that his wish had come true and hers hadn't!

Or had it? she wondered.

She tiptoed to her window and looked down at the turkey pen. It had stopped snowing. A cloud drifted over the face of the moon, dulling the light that washed over the ghostlike drifts piled up in the corners. But even in the dimness she could see the pen was still empty. Her wish hadn't come true. Gobble-de-gook hadn't come back to life.

Sighing sadly, she snuggled into bed and drifted off to sleep, dreaming of the big brown turkey that had been her pet.

Hours later her eyes flew open in alarm. Her pulse was racing and her body was covered in sweat. Had she heard something? What was it? Where had it come from? Was it real or part of her dream?

She sat up in bed and held her breath as she looked around the silent room. Moonlight streamed in through the window, casting an eerie silver glow. Nothing stirred. The row of stuffed animals on top of her dresser looked frozen in time.

Annie sighed. *It must have been my imagination,* she thought, and snuggled back under the covers.

"Gobble, gobble. Gobble, gobble."

Annie sat bolt upright. This time she knew she had heard something. Jumping out of bed, she raced to the window and looked down at the pen.

"Gobble-de-gook!" she squealed. "It's *you!*"

"Gobble, gobble."

Annie rubbed her eyes. *I must be dreaming,* she thought.

Looking again, she shrank back in terror. It wasn't a dream.

It was a nightmare!

Gobble-de-gook's eye sockets were empty. One wing was broken and dangling down his side. Most of his feathers were missing, and tatters of rotting skin hung from his body.

Annie shook her head slowly. She couldn't believe it. There had to be some mistake. Maybe her eyes were playing tricks on her, after all. She unlatched the window and raised it slowly. Maybe if she got a closer look . . .

The moment she stuck her head outside an unbelievable stench filled her nose. "Pew," she said, gagging. It smelled like the dead mouse her mother had found behind their refrigerator last month—only a hundred times worse!

She slammed the window shut. Gobble-de-gook had come back from the dead!

"What have I done?" she whispered as tears rolled down her cheeks.

The turkey was standing in the snow gazing up at her window. Now the pitiful sounds coming from his throat seemed more like a cry for help than a turkey's gobble.

"Squawk, squawk," he cried in a feeble voice. Then he leaned against the pen and raised his head as if he was begging her to come to his rescue.

Annie gasped. "What am I going to do? He'll freeze out in the snow. But—"

Kyle! she thought. *He'll know what to do.*

Her heart was racing as she tiptoed through the dark hallway toward his room. The house was silent except for the tick of the grandfather clock downstairs.

Suddenly a floorboard squeaked underfoot. Annie froze in her tracks and listened, praying that her parents were sleeping soundly.

Ticktock. Ticktock. Ticktock.

She moved on. When she reached her brother's door, she turned the knob, pushed it open, and hurried inside.

"Kyle," she whispered, touching him gently on the shoulder. "Wake up, Kyle. Gobble-de-gook's back!"

Her brother stirred and mumbled something in his sleep that she couldn't understand. He rolled over without opening his eyes.

The turkey's frantic cries were becoming softer but Annie could still hear them through Kyle's bedroom window.

"Kyle!" she said aloud, shaking him harder. "Please wake up!"

This time his eyes opened. He squinted up at her and then scowled. "Whadda *you* want? Don't you know it's the middle of the night?"

"Kyle, listen to me. You've got to look out your window at the turkey pen. Gobble-de-gook's back, but he's . . ." She couldn't finish the sentence. The words stuck in her throat. "Come on, you've got to see for yourself!"

Grumbling, Kyle threw off the bedclothes and stood up.

"Brrrr. It's freezing," he said as his bare feet hit the floor. He wrapped his arms around himself. "This had better be good."

Annie hadn't noticed the cold, but now as Kyle headed for the window, her teeth began to chatter. She knew it wasn't only from the chilly temperature.

"Yikes!" Kyle slapped a hand over his mouth to stifle the sound and pointed the other toward the window. "Did you see . . . I mean, it's . . ."

"It's Gobble-de-gook," Annie said in a loud whisper. "I wished him back to life, but I didn't mean for him to come back this way! What are we going to do, Kyle? We can't leave him down there like that! He'll freeze!"

Kyle shook his head and backed away from the window. His eyes were wide with fright. "Don't look at *me*," he said in a shaking voice. "I didn't have anything to do with this. You're the one who wished him back."

"I know that," Annie insisted. "But I didn't know he'd be . . ." She paused, trying hard to push out the words. "I didn't mean for him to be like *this*. We have to help him. Don't you see? Maybe we can help him get better."

Kyle thought it over for a moment, tossing leery glances out the window at the pitiful bird in the pen below. Annie could almost hear the argument going on in his head.

Finally he sighed. "Okay, you win. We'll give it a try. Here's what we'll do."

Annie moved closer to her brother and listened as he told her his plan.

"We'll get dressed right now and sneak down to the pen. We'll take him out and hide him in the barn. He'll be okay there for the night. There's even some leftover turkey feed out there. Tomorrow's Saturday so we don't have to go to school. When nobody's looking, we'll take him up to our secret cave in the woods and take care of him until he's well again."

"I don't want to hide him in that old cave," Annie said.

"We can't show him to Mom and Dad. Not the way he looks now," said Kyle. "How would you explain it? 'Guess what, Mom and Dad. When I broke the wishbone, I wished for Gobble-de-gook to come back from the dead, and look! My wish came true!'"

Annie sighed. She knew her brother was right. They would have to nurse him back to health and then think of something to tell their parents.

She went to the window and pressed her face against the glass. "Don't worry, Gobble-de-gook," she whispered. "We'll take care of you. You're going to be as good as new."

Gobble-de-gook jerked to attention and tilted his head upward toward the window. Somehow he had heard her.

Chapter

3

Annie rushed to her room to get dressed. She pulled corduroy pants and a ski sweater on over her pajamas. Next came heavy socks, fur-lined boots, her down jacket, and knitted hat and mittens. She took a deep breath to calm down the little prickles of fear that raced up and down her back. She was ready.

Kyle was already in the hall. Together they groped their way down the stairs in the dark. They tiptoed across the family room toward the back door. Trouble was snoring away in his bed.

Some watchdog, Annie thought. *All he ever wants to do is eat and sleep.*

They let themselves out. The snow crunched underfoot as they headed for the turkey pen.

Annie had taken only a couple of steps when she stopped and clamped a hand over her nose. "Pe-yew!" she said, gasping at the putrid smell that assaulted her.

"Ugh! I smell it, too!" said Kyle, making a face. "It smells like something *dead*." He blinked at her. "Uh-oh! Are you sure that *is* Gobble-de-gook?"

Annie nodded, pressing her hand tighter over her nose. "I tod you I wished hib back frob da dead."

"Gross!" said Kyle. "I don't think I want to do this."

"Squawk! Squawk!" The big bird flapped his good wing and limped frantically around the pen, stirring up an even more putrid smelling breeze.

"It's all right, Gobble-de-gook. Pipe down," Annie gasped. "Kyle didn't mean that! Everything's going to be okay."

She frowned at Kyle and said, "Come on. Let's get him into the pen."

But Kyle hung back. His face went pale, and he was staring wide-eyed at Gobble-de-gook.

18

As Annie came closer and unlatched the pen, she understood why.

From the upstairs windows, the turkey had looked awful, but now, as he swept past her and into the yard, he looked even worse.

The eye sockets she had thought were empty weren't empty at all. They were full of writhing, pulsing maggots. Pus oozed from the holes in his rotting flesh. His broken wing dangled from a bloody string of skin. But worst of all was the menacing sound that rose from his throat.

"SQUAAAAWWWWKKK!"

Annie's blood froze. She tried to tell herself that she had never heard the noise before. That it wasn't the same sound Frankenturkey had made when he terrorized them the year before.

No, she told herself. *We ate Frankenturkey. This is Gobble-de-gook! And he's cold. And hungry. And scared!*

She took off for the barn with the scraggly bird slowly hobbling along behind her. She had the heavy barn door open before he could cross the frozen lawn.

"Come on, Kyle. Help me get the feed out," she called in a loud whisper.

Kyle hadn't moved. He was still staring at the turkey, and he looked scared to death.

Snorting in disgust, Annie trudged into the barn. Enough moonlight was streaming in the open door for her eyes to adjust to the darkness. She peered around at all the odds and ends of garden tools and patio furniture. Finally she spotted a burlap bag leaning against a wall in one shadowy corner. The turkey feed!

"Here, Gobble-de-gook. Here, Gobble-de-gook," she called softly as she scattered the grain across the dirt floor.

The turkey was standing in the doorway, a stark black silhouette against the blinding white snow.

Annie sucked in her breath at the sight. Was it really Gobble-de-gook? Why did he look so scary?

Of course he looks scary, she told herself. *He's been dead since last summer, and it's my fault he looks this way.*

"Here, Gobble-de-gook," she called again. "It's okay."

The big bird strutted inside and began pecking at the feed.

"Gobble, gobble," he said softly. Annie

watched in silence as he gobbled up the grain. She prayed that the food would give him strength and help him get back to normal. She wanted him to be the sweet, gentle pet he had been before. And if that happened, wishing on Frankenturkey's wishbone would be the luckiest thing she had ever done.

Chapter

4

I t is *not* Frankenturkey. It's Gobble-de-gook!" Annie insisted. It was the next morning, and she was stomping through the ankle-deep snow toward the barn with Kyle and Jake. "I've told you a hundred times, Kyle Duggan. I know what I wished for on that wishbone!"

"Well, he looks mean enough to be Frankenturkey," said Kyle.

"I can't wait to see him. He sounds totally *gruesome*," said Jake.

Annie didn't try to hide her annoyance at Kyle for inviting Jake Wilbanks over to help sneak Gobble-de-gook out of the barn.

"It's *our* turkey, not *his*," she had protested when Kyle told her he had called Jake.

The year before, Jake had stolen Kyle's lunch money every morning, and one day he had followed Kyle and Annie home from school. That's when he had first seen Frankenturkey, and had run away with his eyes popping out of his head from fright.

After that, Kyle and Jake had worked together to save each other from the anger of the monster bird. Ever since they'd been good friends.

Still, Annie wished Kyle had kept Jake out of it.

"Hey, Kyle, do you think he might really be Frankenturkey instead of Gobble-de-gook?" Jake asked, squinting his beady eyes and peering in through the barn door.

"How could Frankenturkey come back? We ate him!" Annie cut in.

"So? Gobble-de-gook was just as dead. We *buried* him," Kyle snapped back at her. "Besides, it was Frankenturkey's wishbone. Maybe he wanted to come back to life himself and Gobble-de-gook's body was handy."

Annie couldn't think of an answer for that. And anything she said would only make Kyle call her stupid again. She decided to keep

23

quiet for now. She had made a wish, and it had come true, the same as her brother's had. That was all there was to it.

Now she would nurse Gobble-de-gook back to health, and then Kyle and Jake would see once and for all which turkey it really was.

They eased the barn door open and stepped inside, blinking to adjust to the darkness.

"Okay, where is he?" asked Jake.

"Over there," said Kyle, pointing to a dark object. "See how mean he looks? That's got to be Frankenturkey."

The big bird cocked his head and turned his empty eye sockets in their direction. "Squaaawwwkkk!"

Jake's Adam's apple bounced wildly as he stared at the turkey. "He's just as gross as you said. And he *stinks!*" Jake yelled. Suddenly he made a mad dash for the corner of the barn. Annie heard him barfing up his breakfast.

She forgot all about Jake and the smell of rotting flesh as she studied Gobble-de-gook, pecking at his feed. He had a lot more feathers than she remembered. In fact, last night it had seemed to her that he was completely bald. His broken wing wasn't

24

dangling at his side, either. It was tucked tightly against his body.

Is he starting to get well already? she wondered in amazement.

"Gobble, gobble. Gobble, gobble," he seemed to reply.

"Oh, Gobble-de-gook," she whispered joyfully. "I know it's really you. Don't listen to Kyle. Okay?"

"Gobble, gobble," the turkey responded. Annie knew he understood.

"We'd better hurry before Mom and Dad get back," Kyle said.

Saturday was the day Mrs. Duggan did the weekly grocery shopping. Mr. Duggan had left with her, saying he needed to get a haircut and stop by the hardware store. But Annie knew those chores wouldn't take very long.

Kyle told Jake to carry the bag of feed. "I'll bring the chicken wire," he said, "and you"— he turned to Annie—"can bring the turkey, since you're so crazy about him."

"If you think he's Frankenturkey instead of Gobble-de-gook, why are you so willing to help take care of him?" Annie challenged.

Kyle studied the bird. "Look," he said, "I don't know for sure that he's Frankenturkey.

It's just a feeling I have. But I don't know for sure that he isn't, either. As long as there's a chance that he's Gobble-de-gook, I guess I have to go along with taking care of him even if he does gross me out."

Annie peeked out the barn door to make sure the coast was clear. Trouble was in the house, sleeping off his breakfast, and the family's van wasn't back in the driveway yet.

"Come on, Gobble-de-gook. Here, turkey, turkey," Annie called softly.

Gobble-de-gook stopped pecking at the feed and trotted toward the door. He was steadier on his legs than he had been when they led him into the barn the night before.

They crunched through the snow, Annie and Gobble-de-gook in the lead. The turkey seemed to know where he was going as they wound their way through the trees and deep into the woods. A few minutes later they stepped into a clearing where the small cave was carved into the hillside.

Annie caught her breath at the memory of what had gone on there a year ago when Frankenturkey had trapped the three children inside and terrorized them. None of them had been back to the cave since.

Annie, Kyle, and Jake strung the chicken wire across the mouth of the cave, and a few minutes later they had Gobble-de-gook safe in his new pen with plenty of feed scattered around and a dish full of water.

"We have to go now, Gobble-de-gook," Annie said sadly.

The big bird turned his head in her direction. She couldn't be sure, but Annie had the feeling he was trying to look at her with his vacant eyes.

The feeling made her shiver. She looked closer at the bird and did a double take.

Was that a shiny film forming over his maggot-filled eye sockets or was it only her imagination? Maybe it was just the way the light was shining through the trees and glinting off the snow that made it look as if Gobble-de-gook's eyes were coming back. She had hoped with all her heart that they could nurse the big turkey back to health, but she'd never dreamed he'd be able to see again.

Kyle and Jake had already started back toward home. Annie hurried after them, her mind awhirl.

If his eyes really were returning, was it a miracle?

Or more of Frankenturkey's magic?

Chapter

That night Annie tossed and turned in her bed. She could hear the wind moaning outside. For a moment Annie thought she could see the hot glow of Gobble-de-gook's eyes peering out from her open closet. She buried her face in the darkness of her pillow. Soon she began to dream. . . .

Annie was hurrying through the woods toward Gobble-de-gook's pen. She had sneaked away from the house without Kyle because she had an overwhelming feeling that the turkey wanted to see her—*alone*.

Annie had never been in the woods by herself before. It was dark and cold. And spooky. Branches reached out for her like clutching hands. The wind made the trees sway like soulful ghosts. She shivered every time a twig snapped or a squirrel skittered across her path.

She was breathless from fright when she reached the clearing. She squinted into the dark cave, trying to see the turkey.

"Gobble-de-gook?" she called as she cautiously approached the opening. "Are you in there?"

When he didn't answer, she looked around the clearing in a panic. Had something happened to him? Could a wild animal have gotten in and dragged him away? Or worse?

No, she thought instantly. The chicken wire was still strung tightly over the mouth of the cave. Nothing could have gotten inside.

"Gobble-de-gook?" she called again. "Where are you?"

Then she heard it. A faint "gobble, gobble" coming from far back inside the dark cave.

Slowly the big bird waddled out of the shadows toward the wire. Annie's eyes widened in awe. He was beautiful! Just like the old Gobble-de-gook! All of his wounds had healed. His feathers had grown back into the most gorgeous brown plumage she had ever seen. And his eyes were perfect again, too, glittering like jewels in his head.

Annie sucked in her breath. "Oh, Gobble-de-gook! You're as good as new!" she cried as she raced toward him.

But Gobble-de-gook took a step backward.

Annie stopped. "What's wrong?" she asked.

The big turkey dropped his head sadly to one side, and let his wings droop loosely by his sides. Annie thought she saw a tear gleaming in his eye.

Hurriedly she unfastened the wire across the mouth of the cave and rushed inside.

"Oh, Gobble-de-gook, are you okay?" she asked around a lump in her throat.

The big bird slowly raised his head and thrust out his chest. Then with a giant motion he swept both wings forward so that their tips rested on his chest.

Puzzled, Annie reached out and stroked the soft feathers.

"Gobble, gobble. Gobble, gobble."

He leaned toward her, pressing her hand deep inside.

"Gobble, gobble. Squaawwkk!"

"You're trying to tell me something, aren't you, Gobble-de-gook?" Annie asked anxiously.

"Squaawwkk! Squaawwkk!"

She plunged her hand deeper into the feathers until she felt the soft flesh. It was too soft. There was no bone!

At first she didn't understand. "Are you trying to tell me that you're perfect again except for one missing bone?" she asked.

"SQUAAAWWWKKK!" squalled the turkey, hopping up and down and flapping his wings.

Then it dawned on Annie. "The wishbone!" she cried. "You want the wishbone that I wished you back to life on!"

Gobble-de-gook flapped his wings excitedly again.

"Don't worry, Gobble-de-gook! I'll get it for you right now!"

Annie whirled around and raced back to the house. The empty family room seemed strange in the darkness. She dug frantically through the toy box until finally she found the wishbone's broken halves. Grabbing a piece in each hand, she stumbled through the woods again, the cold, wet snow clinging to her bedroom slippers.

Annie was panting breathlessly when she reached the cave.

31

Gobble-de-gook was waiting, pressed up against the wire. His glittering eyes followed her as she hurried through the clearing.

"Here! Here it is!—just like!—just like you wanted!" she cried between gulping breaths. She held the halves of the wishbone out toward the bird.

As he strutted forward, head held high and chest thrust out, Annie felt the two pieces of wishbone wiggle their way out of her hands. She watched in amazement as they hung suspended in the air in front of her and fused together into one big wishbone.

Then with a blinding flash of light the wishbone disappeared into the plumage of the bird's chest.

Annie gasped and stepped back, her eyes wide.

The burst of light had subsided and she was lying in a bed. She sat up slowly and looked around. She wasn't in the woods! She was safe in her own room! In her own bed. "I must have been dreaming," she whispered.

She sank back on her pillow as the dream slowly came back to her. Running through the woods with awful things reaching out for her had been terrifying. Gobble-de-gook had seemed so beautiful and strong. But he had been different in other ways, too. He was louder and more confident than the gentle pet she had mourned for so many months. The wishbone had seemed to bring him new life, while Annie felt more tired than she had ever felt before.

The wishbone! she suddenly thought. Had her dream meant something, after all? Was Gobble-de-gook trying to tell her something?

Annie jumped out of bed. Outside her window, dawn was painting the sky a rosy pink. There was just enough light for her to make her way down the stairs and find the toy box in the corner of the family room. She threw open the lid and started rummaging through it. She could remember tossing the two halves of the wishbone back in the box right after she and Kyle snapped it in half. They had to be there.

Suddenly something wet and cold slapped against her cheek, startling her.

"Trouble!" she cried out loud when she saw the big yellow dog wagging his tail happily beside her. He gave her a silly doggy grin and stuck his nose into the toy box.

With Trouble beside her, Annie pulled out every single thing in the box, but the halves of the wishbone weren't there. She peeked into the catcher's mitt, but there was no bone inside. She pulled the lids off all the games and jigsaw puzzles. No bones there, either. She looked every place there was to look. The wishbone pieces had disappeared.

Frowning, she turned to Trouble. "You didn't eat them, did you, Trouble?" she asked. At the sound of the word "eat" Trouble started bouncing up and down, trying to lead her to the kitchen.

Sighing, Annie put everything back in the toy box and closed the lid. She would ask Kyle at breakfast. Maybe he had taken the wishbone pieces to his room.

My dream probably didn't mean anything, anyway, she thought as she trudged back up the stairs.

Annie climbed back into her soft warm bed and started to snuggle under her covers again when something on the floor caught her eye. She gasped and rolled over to look closer at her fuzzy pink bedroom slippers.

A dead leaf clung to one slipper. But that wasn't all. A glob of snow slowly slid down the side of the other one. It turned to water as it melted on the floor.

Annie's heart was in her throat as she bent down and picked up the slippers. They were soaking wet and icy cold. There was no doubt about it, *someone* had been wearing them out in the snow.

There's only one person who could have done that, Annie thought. *Me! But I didn't go into the woods. It was only a silly dream!*

She rushed to the window and looked down at the snow-covered lawn. There were definitely footprints leading from the back door of the house, across the backyard, and into the woods.

"*My* footprints," she whispered as the frightening truth sank in. "Maybe it wasn't a dream. Maybe I really did take that wishbone out to Gobble-de-gook in his cave in the woods." She wrapped her arms around herself and stared down at the yard below.

Chapter

A little while later Annie looked down at the two fried eggs on her plate. She felt the hairs on the back of her neck stand straight up. The eggs looked like a pair of eyes, staring back at her. And the two link sausages that curved toward each other in the shape of a wishbone made her feel light-headed. Her fork dropped out of her hand and clattered on the table.

"May I be excused?" she asked in a small voice.

Mrs. Duggan turned from the stove and frowned. "But you haven't even taken a bite," she said.

"I—I don't feel very good," Annie said. She

wasn't lying, either. Her stomach felt all jumpy and tense. She didn't think she could keep down even one taste of the runny eggs or sausage.

Mrs. Duggan put down her spatula and came over to feel Annie's forehead.

"I don't think you have a fever," she said. "But maybe you should go back to bed for a while, anyway."

Annie started to get up from her chair when she felt a sharp kick under the table.

When she looked up, Kyle was scowling. "What do you think you're doing? We have to feed the turkey," he muttered from behind his hand.

Annie looked around to see if either of their parents had heard him. Her mother had turned back to the stove, and her father's nose was buried in the sports section of the Sunday paper.

"Come up to my room as soon as you're through eating," she whispered back. "I've got something to tell you, and it's important."

By the time Kyle got to her room, she was having second thoughts about telling him her weird nightmare. Kyle would never believe her. It would be the perfect chance for him to call her stupid again.

"So what'd you want?" he asked, leaning against the door frame. He was wearing his coat and had his ice skates draped over his shoulders.

She looked at him uncertainly. "I was just wondering if you noticed yesterday how fast Gobble-de-gook is getting well."

"Yeah, I noticed. So what?"

"I don't know. I just wondered," she said with a shrug.

Kyle turned to leave.

"Aren't you going to go feed Gobble-de-gook?" she called after him.

"Naw," Kyle replied without turning around. "I'm going to play hockey on the pond behind the Wilbanks'. It's frozen solid."

Annie was horrified. "But he'll starve," she insisted.

"No, he won't. We left him plenty of feed yesterday," said Kyle. "Besides, I wouldn't be caught dead going up to that cave by myself." He turned around and gave her a wicked grin. "Get it? Caught dead with Frankenturkey?" He held his hands in the air like claws and laughed his most hideous monster laugh. Then he ducked into his room.

"He's not Frankenturkey! He's Gobble-de-gook!" she yelled back.

38

Annie lay in bed long after Kyle left for Jake's house. She was eager to go back to the cave and see if Gobble-de-gook really looked as good this morning as he had last night. And she wasn't a scaredy-cat like Kyle, either.

She couldn't explain how Gobble-de-gook had come back to life. Why he was getting well so quickly or even why he had wanted the wishbone. All she knew was she was glad to have her pet turkey back, and she couldn't wait to see him again.

Finally she couldn't lie there any longer. Jumping out of bed, she threw on her clothes and hurried downstairs to find her mother.

"I'm feeling better now. I think I'll go outside for a while," she said.

Mrs. Duggan looked up from the book she was reading and frowned. "Not until you've had some breakfast. I set your plate in the microwave."

Annie took a couple of bites and threw the rest in the garbage. She was too excited to eat. Slipping out the back door, she hurried through the woods toward the cave.

When she got there, Gobble-de-gook was pressed against the chicken wire as if he was waiting for her.

"Gobble, gobble. Gobble, gobble."

Annie took one look at the beautiful bird and felt a rush of love.

"Oh, Gobble-de-gook! You're so gorgeous!" she cried. "I wish we didn't have to hide you up here in the cave. Oh, I wish so much that I could take you home!"

Gobble-de-gook began pecking hard at the ground around one of the poles that held the chicken wire strung tight across the mouth of the cave. Annie watched in amazement as the turkey loosened the ground around the pole, then took hold of the wire fence with his beak and pulled it over.

The big turkey raised his head high in the air and strutted out of the cave, through the trees, and toward the house.

"What are you doing?" she cried. "You can't go back there. What would I tell my parents?"

Gobble-de-gook sped up, and Annie had to run to keep up with him.

"Gobble-de-gook! Come back!"

Suddenly an idea flashed in her mind. There was a way to get him back into his old pen beside the garage. Why hadn't she thought of it before?

"Mom, Dad, look!" Annie cried a few minutes later. She motioned her parents to come to the window and pointed to the backyard where Gobble-de-gook was waddling around in his pen. "I found him in the woods. He looks just like Gobble-de-gook! Can we keep him? Oh, please, *please* say yes!"

Mr. Duggan whistled low. "My, my. He certainly does look like Gobble-de-gook. Where in the world did he come from?"

"The woods," Annie insisted. "I told you I found him. He was just wandering around— lost. He needs a home!"

Her parents exchanged worried glances.

"But what if someone else lost him?" Mrs. Duggan asked. "They might want him back."

"I agree with your mother. Maybe someone was fattening him up for Thanksgiving dinner, the way we fattened up our turkey last year," said her father. "Maybe the bird wandered out of the yard and into the woods. We'd better call around to some of the neighbors and see if anyone is missing a turkey."

Annie sighed in frustration. "I wish you guys wouldn't say that," she grumbled. "I want to keep him and take care of him."

"Of course, dear. I think that's a wonderful idea," Mrs. Duggan said, smiling affectionately at her daughter.

"So do I," said her father. "Finding a turkey just like Gobble-de-gook makes this your lucky day."

Annie blinked at her parents in astonishment. Was she hearing things? They had just said that he probably belonged to someone else and that they should try to find out who lost him. Now suddenly they were saying she could keep him.

It was just like—*magic*!

Chapter

Annie was busy getting Gobble-de-gook settled in his pen when Kyle and Jake came tearing around the side of the house. They were breathless from running, but when they saw the big turkey, they stopped in their tracks and stared.

Jake's mouth dropped open. "What—what happened? I mean, yesterday the sucker was half-dead! And look at him now!"

Kyle shot Annie a questioning look.

Annie nodded to her brother. "I told Mom and Dad that I found him in the woods, and they said we could keep him."

"But how did he get well so fast?" Kyle asked, looking puzzled.

"Yeah," said Jake. "His *eyes* are back and his feathers and— and he doesn't *stink* anymore!"

"I don't know," Annie admitted. "All I know is, it happened."

Just then the back door opened and Mrs. Duggan leaned out.

"Anybody for hot chocolate?" she called.

"No, thanks," Kyle yelled back. "We want to see the turkey."

Their mother went back in, but before she could shut the door, Trouble bounded out into the yard. He perked up his ears when he saw Gobble-de-gook and streaked toward the pen, barking like crazy.

"Stop that barking, Trouble," Annie ordered. "Don't you recognize your old friend Gobble-de-gook? You like him, remember?"

Trouble ignored her. His nose bounced against the ground like a dribbling basketball as he raced back and forth along the front of the pen barking and snarling.

"Trouble!" Annie shouted. "Listen to me."

"Don't be stupid, Annie," grumbled Kyle. "Trouble's probably forgotten all about Gobble-de-gook since last summer. If one human year is equal to seven dog years, then

44

half a year would be three and a half years to him. Do you expect Trouble to remember something that happened three and a half years ago?"

"Yeah," Jake said. "And dogs aren't all that crazy about turkeys, you know. He's just acting like a normal dog."

Annie frowned at the boys. "Well, I wish he'd stop acting like a normal dog when he's around our turkey," she said.

"What do you want him to act like?" Kyle asked sarcastically. "A cat?"

Annie narrowed her eyes at her brother. He was acting all superior again. Just because he was older than she was didn't mean he was smarter.

"Sure," she said defiantly. "I do wish Trouble would act like a cat whenever he's around Gobble-de-gook. So there, smarty!"

Trouble stopped barking. He sat down and began licking his paw.

Annie gulped. "What's the matter, Trouble?" she asked softly.

"Nothing's the matter," said Kyle, shrugging. "He just quit barking, that's all."

Trouble gave his paw a final lick. Then he stood up again and sauntered over to the pen with his tail held straight up in the air. Rubbing against the wire, he began to purr loudly.

"*Trouble!*" Annie and Kyle and Jake cried at the same time.

Ignoring them, Trouble scooted across the snow-packed ground on his stomach, chasing a dead leaf that was blowing across the lawn. He batted it first with one paw and then another, finally pouncing on it and carrying it off in his mouth.

"He really is acting like a cat!" Annie whispered in disbelief. "And all I did was wish . . ." Her mind was spinning so fast that she couldn't get the rest of the words out.

"Let's get out of here!" shouted Kyle. He took off racing toward the house. "Come on, Annie. Come on, Jake."

The three children raced up the stairs and into Kyle's room with Trouble at their heels. When they were all inside, Kyle closed the door and leaned against it.

"I want to know what's going on," he said soberly.

"Yeah," said Jake. "This is weird."

"All I did was wish Trouble would start acting like a cat. And he *did*! How can wishing something make it happen?" Annie questioned.

"Do you think it's got something to do with the wishbone?" Kyle asked. "Weird things have been happening ever since we broke it exactly in half."

Annie nodded slowly. "Yeah, when I wished I could think of some way to bring Gobble-de-gook home from the cave, I suddenly thought of telling Mom and Dad that I found him in the woods."

She paused a second and then went on, her voice rising in excitement. "And then when they wanted to find out if any of the neighbors lost him, I wished they would stop talking like that. That's when they said we could keep him! Don't you see! Whatever we wish for when we're near Gobble-de-gook comes true!"

"It started with Frankenturkey's wishbone," Kyle said. "That must be where the power is."

"Come on," said Jake, making a face. "How can a wishbone from Frankenturkey's carcass make your dog meow?"

"I . . . I don't know," admitted Annie. "It's just that—"

Suddenly Trouble jumped up on Kyle's bed and stretched out, making himself comfortable.

"Get down, Trouble!" Annie yelled. "You know you're not allowed on the beds."

Trouble raised his head and looked at her, but he didn't make any move to get down.

"Trouble! I'm warning you," Annie said. She put her hands on her hips and advanced toward him.

"Arf! Arf!" he barked defiantly. Then he wagged his tail and rolled over on his back the way he always did when he wanted his stomach rubbed.

"He's acting like a dog again," Kyle said. He flopped onto the bed and put his arms around the big yellow dog, nuzzling him happily.

"Trouble's normal, and you know what I think?" asked Jake. "That's the way he's always been. I don't know why he acted like a cat in the backyard, but that other stuff is ridiculous."

"I think you're right, Jake," Kyle said. He sat up on the bed and shook his head. "I know our wishes came true when we broke the wishbone, but the rest is probably just coincidence. That's all it could be. Come on, Annie. Admit it."

Annie glanced out the window and down at Gobble-de-gook, strutting around in his pen. A soft glow in the shape of a wishbone seemed to come from his chest. She squinted hard and looked again, but she couldn't be sure if she really saw something or if she was just imagining things.

"Maybe," she murmured. But why did strange things always seem to happen when they were near Gobble-de-gook?

Chapter

For the next few days Gobble-de-gook acted like a normal turkey, and Annie couldn't see any signs of a glowing wishbone. And Trouble was back to his old routine of sleeping and begging for food. She was beginning to think that Kyle had been right. Gobble-de-gook's coming back to life was scary. Maybe it had caused her to imagine all the rest of the weird things.

Kyle was starting to like Gobble-de-gook, too. Sometimes when they fed him after school, they would let him out of his pen to follow them around the yard the way he had in the old days before he was hit by the truck. Trouble mostly stayed up on the porch when they did that, watching Gobble-de-gook and occasionally letting out a whine. And Kyle was even trying to teach the big bird to fetch a stick. He wasn't having much luck though. The turkey just looked at him and waddled off.

Then after school on the Monday before Thanksgiving, when they went out to feed Gobble-de-gook with Trouble trotting along beside them, it happened again.

"Meeoww."

"Did you hear that?" Annie asked.

"Sure," Kyle said, scowling at her. "But it was you, wasn't it?" he demanded. "You meowed so I'd think it was Trouble."

"I did not!" Annie fired back.

Suddenly Trouble rubbed so hard against Annie that he nearly knocked her over. "Meeoww."

"See? It *was* Trouble. He's acting like a cat again," she insisted.

Kyle dropped to one knee in front of Trouble. Taking his big yellow head in both hands, Kyle said patiently, "You're a dog, Trouble. A *D-O-G*. Now bark."

Trouble blinked lazily and began to purr. The purr was so loud that it made Annie think of the sound their dad's lawn mower made when he cut the grass in the summer.

"Trouble, *bark*!" Kyle said, shaking the dog's head in frustration.

"Meeoww," said Trouble.

Just then Annie heard a car and looked up to see her father pulling the van into the driveway. He was going to park the van in the garage, the way he did every night. He would have to pass the turkey pen on his way to the house. The same thing had obviously occurred to Kyle, too.

"Oh, no! What if he hears Trouble meowing? We've got to get him back in the house." He hurriedly grabbed the dog's collar and starting dragging him toward the back door.

"Sssstt!" hissed Trouble. He reached out a paw, flexed his claws, and jabbed at Kyle.

"Okay, Trouble. Okay, boy," Kyle whispered as he knelt beside the dog and began petting his head. "Just keep quiet until Dad goes into the house, okay?"

Mr. Duggan came out the side door of the garage and headed for the house. Annie held her breath, waiting for him to say hi to them as he walked by. Kyle had his hand wrapped over the dog's mouth.

But their father didn't seem to notice them. He had a glazed look in his eyes as he trudged toward the house.

Suddenly Trouble broke away from Kyle and trotted alongside Mr. Duggan.

"Meeeowwww!"

"Oh, hi, Trouble," Mr. Duggan murmured. He reached down absently and patted the dog on the head. "Come on, boy. Let's go in the house."

Annie and Kyle watched as their father led Trouble in the back door. When the door closed they looked at each other in amazement.

"What's the matter with Dad?" Annie asked. "He didn't even notice when Trouble meowed."

"Beats me," Kyle said. "I'm just glad he didn't. And I hope Trouble changes back into a dog when he gets into the house."

The kids hurriedly spread feed around Gobble-de-gook's pen and filled his water bowl, not even taking time to talk to him. They had to get back into the house to check on Trouble.

The big yellow dog was snoozing in front of the fireplace when they got there, and their parents were deep in conversation on the family-room sofa.

"Wash up for supper, kids," their mother said. "And do it quickly. We have something important to discuss."

Annie couldn't help noticing that she looked worried. "Do you think they know about Trouble?" she whispered to Kyle as they hurried up the stairs.

Kyle shrugged. "Who knows?"

Tension hung in the air as Annie and Kyle sat down at the dinner table. Nobody said anything while the food was passed and plates were filled.

Annie's heart beat fast. She looked at each of her parent's faces. Had they somehow found out about her wish that had brought Gobble-de-gook back from the dead?

Finally Mrs. Duggan set down her water glass and said softly, "I hope you'll understand, children, but we're going to have to eat your new turkey for Thanksgiving dinner."

Annie gasped. "Oh, no!" she wailed. "You can't kill Gobble-de-gook!"

"It isn't Gobble-de-gook, dear," her mother said gently. "You found this turkey in the woods, remember?"

"It is, too, Gobble-de-gook!" Annie insisted. "All you have to do is look at him and you'll see."

"Yeah, we won't eat our pet," Kyle blurted out. "You can't make us!"

Their parents exchanged troubled glances.

"In the first place," Mr. Duggan began slowly, "turkeys look pretty much alike. It's hard to tell one from another, so it would be easy for you to mistake this turkey for your old pet."

"We can tell," Annie said defiantly. "This turkey *is* Gobble-de-gook!"

"Annie, be reasonable. Gobble-de-gook died last summer and he's buried—" Mrs. Duggan began, but their father interrupted.

"That's not the only reason we have to eat the turkey," he said soberly. "Thanksgiving is only a few days away, and the bank where I work is closing. I'm out of a job. It's funny," he said, gazing off in the distance. "I don't know how many times driving to work I've wished I didn't have to go to that office, and now I won't be going back."

He paused and cleared his throat. "Your mother is still going to be teaching school, but without my salary, things are going to be tough for a while. We won't even have a Thanksgiving dinner if we don't eat that turkey out in the pen."

"Okay, then we won't have Thanksgiving dinner, if that's what it takes," Kyle snapped.

"Kyle, I wish you'd try to understand," his mother said, reaching across the table and stroking his hand.

Kyle got a blank look on his face for a moment. Then he shrugged. "Okay, we'll eat him. We'll just have to work extra-hard at fattening him up."

Tears spurted into Annie's eyes. *Oh, no!* she thought. *They want to hurt Gobble-de-gook again. And it's all Kyle's fault!*

Chapter

Annie stormed into Kyle's room right after dinner.

"I can't believe you! What's your problem?" she blurted out.

Kyle looked up from his homework. "Who? Me? What are you talking about?"

"You're always calling me stupid. Well, now *you're* the one who's stupid! How dare you say that eating Gobble-de-gook for Thanksgiving dinner was okay with you? And that we'd have to work extra-hard to fatten him up?"

Kyle gave her a bored look. "Think about it. Dad lost his job. We don't have any choice, unless you want to eat peanut butter and jelly for Thanksgiving. We're just lucky we've got that turkey, if you ask me."

"Kyle, that's so cruel!" Annie wailed. "I love Gobble-de-gook, and I thought you did, too."

"Yeah, and I'm going to love him even more stuffed with dressing," Kyle said, rubbing his hands together and licking his lips.

"Kyle Duggan, I hate you, and I'm never going to speak to you again!" she cried, and stormed out of the room.

Annie grabbed her jacket and flew down the stairs. She heard her mother ask where she was going as she raced out the back door, but she didn't stop to answer. She marched straight to the turkey pen.

The big brown turkey was waddling around the pen and pecking at his food. He looked up when she got near. "Gobble, gobble. Gobble, gobble."

Tears streamed down Annie's face as she reached over the wire and stroked his head. "Oh, Gobble-de-gook. It's awful! Dad says we have to eat you for Thanksgiving dinner. He says we don't have the money to buy another turkey. And that's not all! Kyle says it's okay with him. Can you believe that?"

Gobble-de-gook gobbled softly and leaned against the wire. Annie buried her face in his soft feathers for a moment. When she pulled away, she could feel anger building up in her until she thought she might explode.

"I told Kyle off, but it didn't do any good. It's all his fault. If he had helped me argue with Mom and Dad we might have been able to save you. Now he's ruined everything," she said. She started to cry again.

"I just wish *he* was the one being fattened up for Thanksgiving dinner," she said through gritted teeth. "I wish he was getting fatter and fatter, and you were getting skinnier and skinnier—too skinny to eat! So there!"

Annie gasped and shrank back from the pen in horror as she realized what she had said. "I take it back!" she said quickly. "I didn't mean it. Honest. We fight sometimes, but I don't want anything bad to happen to my brother."

The turkey's beady eyes reflected the red of the sunset as he stared at her.

"I don't want anything to happen to you, either," she added around the lump growing in her throat. "I can't eat you for Thanksgiving dinner! I'll talk Mom and Dad out of it! I promise I will! I'll do anything—"

"SQUAAWWK," the bird screamed angrily and scratched ferociously at the ground. "SQUAAAWWWKKK!"

Annie wheeled around and careened toward the house. She had to find out if Kyle was okay.

She was panting when she burst into the family room, and she almost collapsed with relief when she saw Kyle sitting on the sofa watching television and chomping on a cookie. He hadn't gotten any fatter.

Glancing up, he muttered, "What's the matter with you? You look like you just saw a ghost."

She felt giddy with relief. This time her wish had not come true!

Chapter

The next morning at breakfast Kyle ate four bowls of cereal, barely taking a breath between them. Then he fixed himself seven pieces of toast, dripping with strawberry jam, and crammed them into his mouth as fast as he could. Annie's heart sank as she watched him.

"I'm not even full," he bragged as he downed a third glass of milk. "What else do we have to eat?"

Annie looked down at her own bowl of soggy cornflakes and sighed. The sight of Kyle making a pig of himself had taken her appetite away.

"How about some pancakes and sausages,

Kyle, my boy," Mr. Duggan said in a jovial voice as he came into the kitchen. "Since I've lost my job, I'm going to do the best I can to help your mother around the house. In fact, I'm going to be doing the cooking from now on. Just tell me what you want, and I'll fix it. We've got to put a little meat on those bones before Thanksgiving," he said, and chuckled.

Annie felt her face go pale. Her worst fears were coming true. She looked at Kyle, who was beaming at his father.

"I'll take a double stack of pancakes and, um . . . five or six sausages. Do we have any more orange juice?"

Mr. Duggan nodded. "And how about some hot chocolate with lots of marshmallows?"

Annie slid out of her chair and backed away from the table. She was grateful that neither of them noticed. Once she got out of the kitchen, she raced up the stairs to her parents' bedroom.

"Mom?" she called frantically. "Can I come in?"

"Of course, dear," her mother replied.

Annie's heart was thudding and her pulse was pounding in her ears as she approached her mother. Mrs. Duggan was in front of the mirror, applying her makeup before leaving for school.

Glancing at Annie in the mirror, she said, "Sweetie, is something wrong? You look like you've just seen a ghost."

Annie swallowed hard. Now that she was here, she didn't know what to say. She couldn't just come right out and ask if Kyle was being fattened up for Thanksgiving dinner. But she had to try. Her mother was her only hope.

"It's Kyle, Mom," she began in a quivering voice. "Did you know he already ate four bowls of cereal, seven pieces of toast, and drank three glasses of milk? Now he asked Dad to fix him pancakes and sausages, orange juice, and hot chocolate! I . . . I think something's wrong with him."

"Nonsense," her mother said. "He's just a growing boy."

"But don't you think he'll get fat if he keeps eating like that?" Annie asked cautiously.

"Well, I certainly hope so," her mother replied. "After all, Thanksgiving is only two days away."

"But, Mom!" squealed Annie, shrinking back in horror. "You aren't really fattening him up to eat for dinner, are you? Please say you aren't!"

"Now, Annie," her mother said in her most patient voice. "I know you love your brother, just like you loved your pet turkey last year. But you have to realize that things are different this year."

"KYLE ISN'T A TURKEY!" Annie yelled at the top of her lungs. "There's a perfectly good turkey out in the pen. What's the matter with you?"

Mrs. Duggan turned back to the mirror and began putting on her lipstick. She seemed to have forgotten Annie was even there.

Annie shivered with fear as she stood at her window a moment later and looked down at Gobble-de-gook. He looked so ordinary. So innocent. So sweet and gentle, just like he had been before he was hit by the truck.

"But he *isn't* an ordinary turkey. And he's not innocent, sweet, or gentle," she muttered sadly. "Not anymore. Something awful has happened to him, now that he's got Frankenturkey's wishbone inside him."

He can make wishes come true, but that's not the worst of it, she thought. At first the wishes only came true when the person making the wish was near Gobble-de-gook. But the turkey was becoming more powerful. Gobble-de-gook was starting to make wishes come true even when the wishes were made inside the house. When her mother had wished Kyle would understand that they needed to eat Gobble-de-gook for Thanksgiving, Kyle had suddenly changed his mind.

"And now he's so strong he can make people wish what he *wants* them to!" she whispered to herself, and shivered. She thought about her wish that Kyle was the one being fattened up for Thanksgiving dinner instead of the turkey. She hadn't wanted to make that wish. Something had made her do it.

The whole family must be under Frankenturkey's spell, Annie realized. Still, Kyle knew the terrible secret of Frankenturkey. He knew the awful magic the monster bird had possessed. She had to talk to her brother and make him understand what was going on. She had to make him fight against the turkey's power so that Kyle wouldn't end up becoming their Thanksgiving meal.

By the time she grabbed her coat and books and was ready to leave for the bus stop, Kyle was waiting by the door. He was trying to zip his jacket over his bulging stomach.

"I can't wait for lunch," he said, burping loudly. "Dad made me eight sandwiches." He grinned and pointed to a large brown grocery bag on the floor beside him.

"Kyle Duggan, how can you be such a pig?" Annie cried. "Don't you know Dad lost his job, and we don't have as much money to spend on groceries as we did before?" she said, trying to persuade him to slow down his eating.

"Cool it, Annie," Kyle said. "Dad said I could have anything to eat I wanted. So did Mom. She said I'm a growing boy and I need a lot of food. She even promised to bake me a triple-layer chocolate cake with fudge icing when she gets home from school today."

He finished zipping his jacket, picked up his lunch and his books, and headed out the door.

Annie raced after him. She had to try to get through to him. It was now or never. "Kyle, wait! You've got to listen to me! It's important!"

"So what do you want? Are you going to give me half your lunch?" he said. Sneering, he added, "Naw, you wouldn't do that. You're too stingy."

Annie grabbed her brother's arm, whirling him around to face her. "You've got to stop eating so much," she cried. "Don't you know what's happening? You're the one who's going to be Thanksgiving dinner, not the turkey. Gobble-de-gook made me wish that, and now it's coming true. Can't you see? Mom and Dad are fattening you up!"

Kyle seemed to consider what she was saying for a moment. Then he shrugged. "So what's the problem?" he asked.

Annie replied, "I had a dream that Gobble-de-gook asked for Frankenturkey's wishbone. I got up in the middle of the night and took it to the cave and gave it to him. Ever since, Gobble-de-gook has had Frankenturkey's powers."

Kyle looked at her and scowled. "Birdbrain," he muttered. Then a smile spread across his face. "Birdbrain. Get it? You and Gobble-de-gook and Frankenturkey. You're all birdbrains." He threw back his head and laughed.

Annie felt a spark of anger. Then she remembered that Kyle was in danger. "You've got to listen!" she cried frantically. "Frankenturkey's after us again. He's—" She

67

gasped as a horrible thought popped into her mind. She understood it now. She knew exactly what was happening.

"Kyle, we ate Frankenturkey for Thanksgiving dinner last year. This year he's come back to get *revenge!*

Chapter

Annie thought hard as she followed Kyle down their road to the spot where the school bus picked them up. What was she going to do? Her parents couldn't see what was happening to themselves and to Kyle. And Kyle seemed not to care at all that he was going to be the main course for the family's Thanksgiving dinner. But she had to keep trying.

"Kyle, you've got to listen," she said, catching up with him again. "I'm sure it's Frankenturkey that's causing you to act this way. Don't you see? His spirit is in Gobble-de-gook's body!"

"Hey, that Frankenturkey. He's one cool

dude," Kyle said, grinning and giving Annie two thumbs-up.

Annie let out a snort of exasperation. It was no use. And it was all her fault for wishing Gobble-de-gook back to life in the first place. Tears came to Annie's eyes. She sniffed and wiped them away with the back of her hand.

But is it all my fault? she asked herself.

What am I going to do? she wondered as she watched Kyle stop at the corner. He set the big grocery bag on the ground, opened it, and took out one of the sandwiches.

"Man, I wish I had a glass of milk to wash this down." Kyle stuffed the thick ham-and-cheese sandwich into his mouth. Then he started rummaging around in the bag again. "And some chips. I wonder why Dad didn't put any chips in my lunch."

Annie couldn't bear to watch her brother eat. If only she could think of something to do. Then she noticed Jake wasn't at the stop yet.

She felt a sudden ray of hope. That was it! Jake hadn't been fooled by Frankenturkey. He'd help her find a way to stop what was going on.

Just then the school bus came in sight. Annie looked around, expecting to see Jake running to catch up, but he was nowhere to be seen.

Rats! she thought as she climbed onto the noisy bus. *Maybe he took an earlier bus. Or maybe his parents drove him to school. He'd just better be there today.*

When she got to school she wandered around the yard looking for Jake.

Jonathan Bergman, Eric Galvan, and Jason Hart were standing by the bike rack. "Have any of you seen Jake Wilbanks this morning?" she asked.

"Uh-uh," said Jonathan, shaking his head. "I haven't seen him. Have you guys?"

The other two boys said no as well.

"Thanks," murmured Annie.

She asked several other kids if they had seen him, but no one had.

All morning she could hardly sit still at her desk. Twice her teacher, Ms. Gilhooley, called on her, but Annie hadn't even heard the question. She considered telling the teacher about what was going on at home, but she knew how ridiculous it would sound. She couldn't just walk up and say, "My brother and I made a wish on the wishbone of a monster turkey named Frankenturkey that we ate for dinner last Thanksgiving. Now he's getting revenge by making my parents cook Kyle for Thanksgiving dinner this year." Ms. Gilhooley would think she had lost her mind.

At lunchtime Annie rushed to the cafeteria. Kyle was already there. The table in front of him was piled with sandwich wrappers, and kids were staring at him as he stuffed two Twinkies into his mouth at the same time.

She looked desperately around the cafeteria. Jake was not there.

Suddenly a feeling of dread came over her. Had Frankenturkey figured out that she was going to ask Jake for help and done something to him, too? Had the big turkey's power grown so strong that it could tell what she was thinking? Annie shivered at the thought.

The rest of the day was a total loss for Annie. She tried to listen to Ms. Gilhooley, but she couldn't get her mind off Jake. Jake and his parents had eaten Thanksgiving dinner at the Duggans' the year before. Was Frankenturkey going to take vengeance on Jake's family, too? *Were the Wilbanks going to have Jake for their Thanksgiving dinner?*

When the school bus pulled up at their stop later that day, Annie hit the ground running.

Instead of heading for home, she ran down the road toward Jake's house. She was panting and gasping for breath when she reached it and banged on the door.

Moments passed. No one answered.

Annie banged again harder.

Finally it opened. She stepped back in shock. Jake was standing there with a package of cookies in one hand and a bag of potato chips in the other.

Chapter

12

"What's the matter with you?" Jake asked. "What're you staring at?"

"You're . . . you're eating!" said Annie.

Jake looked at the cookies in his left hand and then the potato chips in his right hand and raised an eyebrow quizzically. "So what? People eat all the time, you know."

"But they don't eat two things at once!" she insisted.

"I was just trying to decide whether I wanted something sweet or something salty when you started pounding on the door," said Jake. "I think I'll have the chips. Come on in." He turned and headed back to the kitchen.

"Why weren't you at school today?" Annie asked as she rushed after him.

"Godda culd," Jake said, glancing at her out of the corner of his eye.

"You didn't sound like that when you answered the door," Annie said. She stopped when she realized from the look on his face that Jake was faking it.

"Jake Wilbanks, you are not sick at all," scolded Annie.

"Doesn't hurt for a guy to have a day off from school now and then," said Jake. A wide grin spread across his face. "And I do too have the sniffles. See?" He made a disgustingly loud sniffing noise.

Annie shook her head. "Jake, I need to talk to you."

"Go on," he said, opening the bag and taking out a handful of potato chips.

"Kyle had four bowls of cereal, seven pieces of toast, pancakes, sausages, three glasses of milk, juice, and hot chocolate for breakfast and eight sandwiches for lunch," she said, her voice rising. "This morning he could hardly zip his coat. He's eating everything in sight, and he's going to get positively fat."

"So he likes to eat. So what?" Jake said.

"So what?" Annie asked incredulously. "I'll tell you so what! Frankenturkey made me *wish* Kyle would get fat."

"You're crazy," protested Jake. "No one can make someone get fat by just wishing it."

"Well, I did. And now my parents are going to cook Kyle for Thanksgiving!" Annie wailed.

Jake stopped eating and shook his head. "You really are crazy," he said, his mouth stuffed with chips.

"Didn't I wish Gobble-de-gook back to life?" she challenged.

Jake didn't answer.

"And didn't I wish Trouble would act like a cat when he was around the turkey?" she went on.

"Those had to be tricks," Jake said glumly.

"No, they weren't," Annie insisted. "You know how powerful Frankenturkey was before. Now he's back, and he's stronger than ever. I need help, Jake. We've got to save Kyle."

He stared at Annie for a moment. "I'll help you," he said. "But I still think you're nuts."

Annie smiled at him. "I don't care what you think, as long as you come with me."

When Annie and Jake walked into the Duggans' house a few minutes later they found her father leafing through a bunch of cookbooks, which he had spread out all over the kitchen counter.

"I'm glad you kids are here," he said. "I'm looking up stuffing recipes. Here's a good one." He raised his finger in the air. "How does stuffing made from corn bread, walnuts, and curry sound? The recipe calls for low-fat margarine and a cup of nonfat yogurt. It's got to be good for you."

He gave them a questioning look, but before Annie could say a word, he was pointing to another recipe.

"Or what about oysters, stale bread moistened with clam juice, and anchovies. Sound different? Gosh, I didn't know there were so many good-sounding Thanksgiving recipes." Mr. Duggan grabbed another cookbook and started thumbing through it.

"See, what did I tell you?" Annie whispered to Jake.

"Your dad's cooking. Big deal," Jake said. "Where's Kyle, anyway?"

Annie glanced around the kitchen. She was surprised Kyle wasn't there, consuming more food. Then she noticed the pantry door ajar.

"Kyle? Are you in there?" she asked, pulling it open.

"Yeah, and, man, am I starved!"

Annie shrank back in horror. Kyle was sitting in the middle of the pantry floor with the can opener in one hand and a can of green beans in the other. Empty cans of vegetables and fruit were scattered around him. While Annie and Jake watched in amazement, Kyle opened the can and downed the contents in one big gulp. Then he tore open a package of spaghetti and crammed the long pieces of uncooked pasta into his mouth.

"Sheese!" Jake said. He was standing beside Annie, staring bug-eyed at Kyle. "What's going on?"

Kyle looked up at his friend and tried to smile. But his cheeks were bulging and spaghetti stuck out of his mouth like porcupine quills. In the blink of an eye he had chewed and swallowed the whole box and was grabbing for something else.

"Here, Jake, try this. You'll love it," he said, handing Jake a box of strawberry cake-mix. "I just ate the double Dutch chocolate mix a few minutes ago. It was awesome!"

Jake stood stone-still. When he didn't take the mix, Kyle tore open the box and scooped out a handful, popping it into his mouth. "See? This is all you have to do," he said. "Wow, that's really good," he added, taking another scoop before thrusting the box toward Jake.

Jake took the mix, but he didn't eat it. Instead he gave Kyle a frightened look. "Are you okay?" he asked in a trembly voice.

"Sure," said Kyle as he opened a bottle of vinegar and drank it down. "Just a little hungry, that's all."

"Kyle," Mr. Duggan called from behind them. "Come here a minute. I want to see if you'll fit in the oven or if I'll have to get the gas grill out of the barn."

"Sure, Dad," Kyle said happily. He lumbered to his feet and started waddling across the kitchen toward the stove. "But I'd rather be cooked outdoors on the grill. It would make it seem more like the Thanksgivings we used to have when we lived in Florida."

Suddenly Jake lunged for Kyle and tackled him to the floor.

"What's the matter with everybody?" Jake yelled. "Have you all gone crazy?"

Kyle managed to wriggle out of Jake's grasp. "No, stupid," he snapped. "We're getting me ready for Thanksgiving dinner."

Chapter

"**C**ome outside where we can talk," Annie whispered.

Jake nodded and followed her out into the backyard. Seeing the door open, Trouble jumped up with a wag of his tail and went out with them.

"I can't believe it," said Jake, shaking his head. "This is just a terrible nightmare, right?"

"If you think it's a dream, go ahead and pinch yourself and see if you wake up," said Annie.

Jake raised his forearm and took hold of a piece of flesh between his thumb and forefinger and squeezed hard. "Ouch!" he said, frowning and rubbing the spot. He sighed and looked glumly at Annie. "I guess it's not a dream, all right. What are we going to do?"

"I was hoping you'd have an idea," said Annie. "I know Frankenturkey got into Gobble-de-gook's body when I wished that Gobble-de-gook would come back from the dead. But Frankenturkey couldn't make people wish bad things until he tricked me into giving Gobble-de-gook his old wishbone."

"What did he do with it?" asked Jake.

"It's in his chest," said Annie.

"How did he—oh, never mind," Jake said. "I don't want to hear how he got it inside him."

"I don't know, anyway," Annie admitted. "But if we're going to save Kyle, we've got to get the wishbone away from Frankenturkey and break the spell of the wish. The only trouble is, I don't know how."

"Steal it when he's not looking," Jake said.

"It's not like picking a pocket," said Annie, giving him a look of disgust. "It's inside his body, remember?"

"We've got to catch him and kill him," Jake said. "Then we can cut him open and take the wishbone back."

"We can't do that, Jake," Annie said. "If we

try to catch him, he'll make us wish awful things. He might even make each of us wish the other was dead. We've got to trick him into thinking we're on his side."

Suddenly an idea popped into her head. Annie grinned.

"What?" Jake asked.

"What do you think of this? Let's make Frankenturkey think we want to make sure he doesn't get eaten for Thanksgiving. I'll take him up to the cave as if I'm going to hide him there. You'll be on the hill above the entrance. There's a pile of rocks up there. When he's inside the cave, I'll give you a signal, and you push the rocks down the hill. They'll fall over the cave entrance and trap Frankenturkey inside."

Jake squinted at her. "That's the same idea I just had."

Annie felt like sticking her tongue out at him. He and Kyle might be friends now, but he hadn't changed much since the days when he was a bully. Still, even if Annie didn't like him, she did need his help.

"Once he's trapped, we'll work on the next part of the plan—how to get the wishbone back," Annie said. "I'll give you a head start so you can get to the cave before we do."

She watched Jake run into the woods and disappear among the trees. She gave him ten minutes. Then she took a deep breath for courage and headed toward the turkey pen.

This had better work, she said to herself.

When she reached the pen she did her best to smile. It broke her heart to know that under Gobble-de-gook's soft brown plumage lurked the spirit of Frankenturkey.

"Hi, Frank . . . er, Gobble-de-gook," she said softly, wishing it really were Gobble-de-gook she was speaking to. "How are you today, you beautiful bird?"

The big turkey raised his head and stared at her with beady red eyes. "Squawk!"

"You know how much I love you, Gobble-de-gook," Annie crooned, and moved closer to the pen. She felt tiny goose bumps forming on the backs of her arms.

Frankenturkey inched away and turned his head, giving her a suspicious look. "Squuaawwk!"

It took everything Annie had to force herself to reach out and undo the latch on the gate.

"I want to make sure you don't get eaten for Thanksgiving, Gobble-de-gook. Even though we're planning to have my brother Kyle for dinner, he's getting so big that he's having trouble fitting into the oven. If he gets much bigger, Mom and Dad might decide to eat you instead."

The turkey let out a ferocious squawk, and Annie jumped back in fear.

"And that's not all," she said quickly. "Someone else might steal you for their dinner. You know turkeys get stolen all the time. We wouldn't want that to happen, would we?" She tried to sound as reassuring as possible.

"Just to be on the safe side, I'm going to take you up to the secret cave again. You'll be safe there until after Thanksgiving."

The big turkey seemed to relax and moved back into the center of the pen. Annie opened the gate and Frankenturkey came strutting out as if he owned the world.

"Meow."

Annie looked behind her.

Trouble was sitting nearby, watching.

"Here we go," she said, scooping up a handful of corn from the bag inside the cage. She started dropping kernels as she walked toward the woods. Frankenturkey followed her, pecking at the feed. Trouble walked behind them.

85

Annie led the tiny parade up the hill and into the woods, dropping kernels of corn as she went. The turkey was right behind her, picking each one up, and Trouble followed, meowing loudly. She pulled her jacket close around her as she passed the trees, remembering how the branches had grabbed for her.

It wasn't long before she came into the clearing in front of the cave. She glanced up at the hill just as Jake ducked down behind a big boulder. She looked quickly at Frankenturkey to see if he had spotted Jake, too. The turkey was too busy pecking at the ground.

"Here we are," Annie said loudly enough for Jake to hear. "We're at the cave where you'll be safe and sound, my pretty turkey. Go on in."

The bird hesitated. He squinted his beady red eyes and looked at Annie.

"Go on," urged Annie. "Go on in, Gobble-de-gook. It's for your own good." She pushed the bird toward the cave.

Frankenturkey pushed back and craned his neck to see what was in the shadowy cave.

"There's nothing in there to be afraid of," Annie reassured the bird. "You've been in there before."

Frankenturkey backed away.

"Fran . . . ! Er, I mean Gobble-de-gook, there's nothing to be afraid of. Please go on in. You'll just have to stay there until Thanksgiving is over, and then I'll bring you back to your pen."

Suddenly Frankenturkey's breast started swelling, and Annie could see the wishbone burning bright red in his chest. He didn't believe her. He sensed a trap.

"Trouble, you go into the cave and show him there's nothing to be afraid of," Annie ordered.

But Trouble sank to the ground and began licking an invisible spot off his paw.

"Trouble!" Annie shouted in exasperation.

Trouble continued to ignore her. He was behaving like a cat again! Totally independent. Why couldn't he be a dog right now and obey her command?

"Go on, kitty, kitty." She reached down and shooed him toward the cave.

Trouble gave her an angry look as he got to his feet. Then he flattened his ears and raised his tail and took his time sauntering into the cave and then back out.

Annie breathed a sigh of relief. "See,

Gobble-de-gook? There's nothing to be afraid of in there."

The turkey's glittering eyes surveyed the shadowy cave again. Then he strutted toward it and stepped inside.

Annie glanced up at Jake, who was waiting overhead behind the rocks.

"NOW!" she shouted.

Chapter

14

J ake heaved a shoulder against the largest boulder. It moved slightly and then settled back. He shoved again. Annie could hear him grunt, then the big rock toppled forward. It came thundering down the hill, bouncing off other boulders and slamming into the ground in front of the cave.

Annie heard a loud "SQUAWK!" and saw Frankenturkey dashing toward the mouth of the cave. But he wasn't fast enough.

More rocks came tumbling down the hill, banging against each other. They bounced off the top of the cave opening, thudding and piling up in front of the entrance and raising a huge cloud of dust.

The pile grew higher and higher. Annie watched in fascination as the mouth of the cave disappeared until it was completely sealed off.

She stood coughing in the billows of dust caused by the small avalanche and listened for sounds inside the cave.

Nothing. Complete silence.

She tiptoed closer. Was Frankenturkey dead? Maybe one of the rocks had hit him. Or he had smothered in the cloud of dust.

Just then Jake came sliding and bouncing down the hill.

He was yelling, *"Did it work? Did it work?"*

"Shhh!" Annie cautioned. "I think so," she whispered. "I mean, he's trapped in the cave, and I don't hear any sounds. He could be dead."

Jake cautiously put his ear to one of the rocks.

"I don't hear anything, either," he said.

They stood watching and listening as the minutes ticked by. Not a sound came from inside the cave.

Suddenly Annie had a feeling of jubilation. She couldn't believe it had been so easy. Frankenturkey was captured and probably dead. If that were true, they could get the wishbone back and break the magic spell. Then he wouldn't hurt her family anymore, and Kyle wouldn't be their Thanksgiving dinner.

Annie hugged herself. She grabbed Trouble by the front paws and stood him up, dancing around. "What a wonderful kitty or dog or whatever you are! You helped save Kyle's life," she sang.

She looked around for Jake. He was standing in front of the cave with a weird expression on his face. He looked like he was choking.

She ran to him. "Jake! What's wrong?" she shouted.

"I . . . I wish . . ." gurgled Jake.

Annie looked at him in horror. His face was turning purple, and he was holding his hand over his mouth, trying to stop the words from coming out.

She stared wide-eyed at the pile of boulders in front of the cave. It was happening again! Why hadn't she thought of it? If Frankenturkey's power could reach from the barn into the house, it could certainly reach the short distance from the cave to where Jake was standing. And it meant . . . it meant . . . *Frankenturkey was alive!*

"I wish Frankenturkey . . . !"

"Jake, NO!" Annie screamed. "Don't say it!" She grabbed his arm, trying to pull him away from the cave.

"I wish Frankenturkey wasn't in . . ." Jake was pressing both hands over his mouth hard, trying to shove the words back down his throat. His eyes were wide. Sweat poured down his face. He looked terrified.

"NO, NO, Jake!" Annie screamed. "He isn't dead! Let's get out of here! Run!"

She clutched his arm tighter and yanked hard. "Oh, *please!* Don't let him do it to you!"

But Jake wouldn't budge. He gagged, and the rest of the words came tumbling out. "*I wish Frankenturkey wasn't in that cave!*" He turned to Annie as a look of shock spread over his face.

Slowly he took his hands away from his mouth and stared at the huge pile of stones. "Oh, no! What did I do?" he muttered.

They watched in horror as the rock on the very top teetered, settled back, and then teetered again. Suddenly it came loose, tumbling down and landing at their feet.

Then one by one other stones came loose. They rolled down the little mountain of rocks until there was a huge thundering mass hurtling down.

"Look out!" shrieked Annie. She jumped aside, pulling Jake after her. Trouble scampered away into the underbrush.

The rocks tumbled and smashed and crashed against one another, raising a cloud of dust.

Finally, when all was still and the dust was settling, Annie dared to look at the cave opening. Her worst nightmare had come true. The entrance was completely clear, and standing just inside was Frankenturkey! His wings were spread wide, his red eyes glowing like vicious hot coals. And the wishbone in his breast pulsed ominously.

Annie shrieked and ran back down the path toward home. She could hear Jake's footsteps pounding behind her.

And she could hear the wild flapping of wings.

Chapter

Annie didn't stop running when she reached her backyard.

She knew no one at her house would be able to help. They were all under Frankenturkey's power. She had to find someone else.

"Come on, Jake," she said breathlessly. "Let's go to your house and talk to your parents. They're the only ones left to turn to."

"NO!" shouted Jake, stopping in his tracks. "What if Frankenturkey follows us and hurts them, too?"

"Come on, Jake!" Annie cried. She tugged on his sleeve. "We've got to take the chance. It's the only hope we have. Please hurry."

Reluctantly Jake followed her up the lane

toward his house. "This had better work," he grumbled.

Annie glanced back over her shoulder as she ran. Frankenturkey was nowhere in sight. She tried not to think about what might be going on at home. She hoped Frankenturkey wouldn't take out his rage on her parents or Kyle while she was gone.

"Faster!" she yelled, pumping her legs as hard as she could. "We don't have much time!"

They ran up the winding driveway and collapsed against the porch, puffing and panting. To Annie it seemed like days ago that she had pounded on this very front door and had convinced Jake to go to her house to see what was happening to Kyle. But it had only been a couple of hours. Now Frankenturkey was on the rampage, and she was almost out of hope that she could stop him.

Jake pushed open the door, and they hurried inside.

"MOM! DAD!" he shouted at the top of his lungs. "Anybody home?" The only answer was silence.

They ran from room to room, but the house was empty.

"Mom! Dad! Where *is* everybody?" he cried.

Then turning to Annie, he said, "Mom was here when I left, and Dad should be home from work by now. I can't understand why they aren't here."

Annie glanced around in desperation, looking for anything that might give them a clue to the Wilbanks' whereabouts.

"Maybe they left you a note," she cried. "My mom always sticks them up on the fridge."

"Mine, too," said Jake.

They scrambled to the kitchen. Sure enough, a small square of paper was fastened to the front of the refrigerator by a magnet.

Jake grabbed it. "It says—oh, no!" His eyes were wide with alarm. "It says they've gone to your house!"

Annie grabbed the note out of Jake's hand. Her heart was pounding as she read the message.

Jake,

The Duggans called and asked us to stop by for a few minutes. We shouldn't belong.And of course you're welcome to come over, too, and see Kyle and Annie.

Love, Mom

Annie looked up and met Jake's horror-filled eyes. "They're at *my* house?" she whispered in amazement.

Jake didn't answer. He was streaking out the door.

Annie raced after him, not even bothering to close the door behind her. Her lungs screamed and her side throbbed with pain as she headed down the road toward home. She didn't know how much longer she could run.

It can't be too late! she thought desperately. *It just can't!*

The Wilbanks' green sedan was parked in the driveway when Annie and Jake staggered into the yard. The house looked quiet, and smoke curled from the chimney the way it always did. Annie paused at the edge of the lawn and pulled Jake to a stop beside her.

"What are you doing?" Jake demanded. "I've got to see if my parents are all right." He jerked free and headed for the door.

"Wait," said Annie. "Everything looks okay, but let's check it out, anyway. We should sneak around the side of the house and see if Frankenturkey's in the pen."

Jake grudgingly followed. The two children

tiptoed around the side of the house and peered into the backyard.

Frankenturkey was in the pen. He was gobbling softly and pecking at the feed on the ground.

"He's acting like nothing ever happened," Jake said in amazement. "I know we didn't dream up that stuff at the cave."

"He's acting just like Gobble-de-gook," Annie said sadly. She felt tears gathering in her eyes at the sight of the beautiful brown turkey.

"But he isn't Gobble-de-gook," Jake said. "Come on. Let's go in the front door so he won't see us."

Annie knew Jake was right. But it made her sad to know that the evil Frankenturkey was using Gobble-de-gook's body.

When Annie opened the door and led Jake inside she could hear cheerful voices coming from the family room. *At least it doesn't sound like anything's wrong,* she thought hopefully.

"Hi, everybody," she said, stepping into the room.

All four of the adults looked up from where they sat in a circle. In the center, on the floor, sat Kyle.

"Oh, there you are, you two," Annie's mother said, smiling. "We were wondering where you'd gone to."

"We were playing in the woods," said Jake.

Annie stared straight at Kyle. "Yeah, in the *cave*," she said urgently.

She hoped that the mention of the cave would remind her brother of Frankenturkey and bring him out of the trance he was in. But if Kyle noticed what she said, he didn't show it.

"Jake, the Duggans have invited us for Thanksgiving dinner with them again this year," Mrs. Wilbanks said happily. "Isn't that wonderful? I'm going to bring my sweet potato casserole and a salad."

"Thanks . . . Thanksgiving dinner?" Jake asked in a faltering voice. He looked frantically from one of his parents to the other.

"That's right, son," Jake's father said. "And hasn't Kyle been fattened up nicely?" Mr. Wilbanks reached down and poked at Kyle's round belly. "He's going to be delicious."

Annie shook her head in disbelief. Frankenturkey had gotten to the Wilbanks, too. Now he was getting revenge on everyone who had eaten him last year.

"Wouldn't you really rather have turkey?" she pleaded. "There's one out in our pen that would be perfect."

"Of course not," her mother said indignantly. "He's too scrawny. Kyle is much plumper. In fact, it's almost time to get him ready to cook. That's why your father is borrowing Mr. Wilbanks' ax."

Annie saw for the first time that a gleaming ax was leaning against her father's chair. She was vaguely aware that her mother was saying something about their own ax being too dull to use, but she didn't want to listen. Her mind was spinning.

Suddenly Jake rushed forward, grabbing the ax and waving it over his head. "You aren't going to hurt my friend!" he shouted. "I won't let you."

Annie gasped. "Jake! What are you doing?"

He threw her a triumphant look. "I'm going to kill the turkey!" he said, charging out the back door and toward the pen.

"**N**o, Jake!" Annie shouted. "Don't go near him! You know what will happen! He'll make you wish for something horrible, and it will come true!" She wanted to run after him, but she didn't dare.

"What does he think he's doing?" her father demanded. "We don't want to eat that puny little bird."

"Such a skinny little thing," Mrs. Wilbanks said, nodding. "If you ask me, it would be too tough to chew."

"But he's—" Annie started to argue but stopped in midsentence. It wouldn't do any good. And now she remembered why. When Frankenturkey had made her wish for Kyle to get fatter and fatter, she had also wished that the turkey would get skinnier and skinnier. Now that Mr. and Mrs. Wilbanks had come within reach of Frankenturkey's power, they were all under his spell. Even though he was still big and beautiful like Gobble-de-gook, he had made them think that he was just a pitiful little bird.

Her thoughts jumped back to Jake, and she ran to the window. He was creeping stealthily toward the pen, holding the ax high above his head.

"Here, turkey. Here, turkey, turkey," she could hear him crooning.

Frankenturkey seemed to be asleep in the far corner of the pen. His eyes were closed, and his beak rested on the soft feathers of his breast.

"I'm going to get you, turkey, turkey. Just you wait and see," Jake sang softly.

Annie hung back as long as she could. Finally she couldn't stand it any longer. She had to stop Jake before Frankenturkey hurt him.

"Come on, everybody," she said as she headed out the door. "We can't let Jake kill that poor defenseless turkey."

"That's right!" Mr. Wilbanks said, springing up off the sofa and hurrying after her. "Jake, you get back in here this instant."

The others followed, too, muttering angrily.

"Listen to your father, Jake," Mrs. Wilbanks warned.

Jake ignored them and kept advancing on the pen. "Come here, you stupid bird, and take what's coming to you."

He unlatched the pen and swung open the gate. Still, Frankenturkey didn't open his eyes.

Chills ran up Annie's spine. *He's not really asleep,* she thought frantically. *He's playing possum, waiting for Jake to get near before he attacks.*

Suddenly she caught another movement out of the corner of her eye. Kyle was coming out of the house and waddling across the backyard as fast as his fat body would allow.

"Wait, Jake. You've got the wrong bird!" he pleaded.

Kyle hurried to the low stump where Mr. Duggan always chopped wood for the fireplace and sank to his knees.

"I'm the one you really want to kill," he said, lying down and stretching out across the stump.

Annie heard a scream of terror and knew it must be coming from her. She raced toward her brother, but eight clutching hands grabbed her and held her back. She watched in horror as Jake turned and marched slowly to the stump. Then he raised the ax and poised it directly over Kyle's neck.

"Go ahead! Go ahead!" the grown-ups chanted.

The ax glinted red in the setting sun as the moment seemed frozen in time. Not a breeze stirred, not a bird called. Then Frankenturkey opened his eyes. He rose majestically and strutted to Jake's side.

A smile crossed Jake's face as he began to speak. "I wish that every single person who eats Kyle for Thanksgiving dinner will get sick and die."

Chapter

"**S**TOP!" shouted Mrs. Duggan.

Jake froze with the ax gripped in both hands over his head. Everyone turned and looked at Annie's mother in surprise.

Annie's heart leaped with joy. Was it possible? Had her mother been able to get out from under Frankenturkey's power? Had the sight of her son about to have his head chopped off finally broken the spell Frankenturkey had put on everyone but Annie?

Mr. Duggan turned to his wife and frowned. "What's the problem?"

"We simply can't do this!" she said.

"Why not, dear?" asked Mrs. Wilbanks. "His

head has to be chopped off and he has to be stuffed before he can be put on the grill."

"But Thanksgiving isn't until the day after tomorrow," Mrs. Duggan said sadly. "And I'm afraid we don't have nearly enough refrigerator space to keep him. He'll spoil!"

"Oh my, yes!" exclaimed Mrs. Wilbanks. "She's right. We can't eat tainted meat. That would be dreadful."

"Hmmm," Annie's father said, stroking his chin. "I guess we'll just have to wait until tomorrow."

"No fair!" shouted Kyle. "I want you to do it now! Go on, Jake, chop my head off."

Jake looked from one adult to another for instruction.

"No!" Annie shouted. "Mom's right. Just think how terrible he would taste. We might all throw up at the dinner table if we eat Kyle and he's spoiled."

"Yuck!" Jake said, making a face.

"I'm afraid she's right," Mr. Duggan said. "It would make a terrible mess, and since I've taken over the household chores these days, I certainly don't want to be the one to clean it up." He sighed deeply. "Jake, put down the ax. You can chop Kyle's head off tomorrow."

"It's not fair," grumbled Kyle.

Annie let out a huge sigh of relief as Jake lowered the ax.

Everyone headed back toward the house with Kyle angrily straggling behind.

Annie turned and stared at Frankenturkey. The big bird was peacefully scratching and pecking at the ground inside his pen.

Why aren't my parents and the others able to see what is happening? she wondered. *How has Frankenturkey convinced them that cooking Kyle for Thanksgiving is the perfect thing to do?*

Tears ran down Annie's cheeks. It was Gobble-de-gook's body, and she had refused to believe the spirit of Frankenturkey had taken it over. But it had. It had turned her beautiful pet into a monster. Gobble-de-gook had been so sweet and loving. He would hate it if he knew what Frankenturkey was doing to her and her family. If only it had been *his* spirit in the body instead of Frankenturkey's. She rubbed away the tears with her hands.

But it *wasn't* Gobble-de-gook's spirit, and she didn't know what to do. She didn't know where to turn.

There was no one on earth who would

believe her if she told them her parents and the Wilbanks were going to have *stuffed Kyle* for Thanksgiving. She could hardly believe it herself. She was trapped in a nightmare and couldn't wake up. She turned and trudged after the others.

That night Annie couldn't sleep. She tossed and turned and got tangled in her bedcovers. She pounded her pillow and chewed on the corner of her pillowcase as her mind whirled in a million directions. What could she do to save her brother? *What could she do?*

The moon streaming in through her window was almost as bright as daylight. Annie got out of bed, slipped her robe over her shoulders, and went over to the window, pulling back the curtains. Down below, in the pen next to the garage, she could see a dark form.

It was Frankenturkey.

It is strange how the big bird is able to cast his spell over everyone except me, she mused. For a reason she didn't understand she was free from his powers. It was true that the turkey had forced her to make terrible wishes, but now she understood what was happening and was fighting back. The others weren't. They were in a trance. Kyle actually loved the idea of being the main course for Thanksgiving dinner. And her father was excited about cooking him on the barbecue grill. Why was she different?

At that moment, Frankenturkey looked up at her window. His eyes burned like small fires in the night as he stared up at her.

Annie shivered and pulled her robe close around her.

How had she let the bird fool her into thinking he was Gobble-de-gook, the pet bird she loved? It was Gobble-de-gook's body down there in the pen, but the brain was Frankenturkey's. And she hated him for what he was doing to her family.

The two spots of red flared in the pen below.

Annie gritted her chattering teeth and put on her slippers. She couldn't let them cook her brother for Thanksgiving without trying one last time to save him.

She opened the back door and peered nervously out into the backyard. Moonlight splashed over the snow, turning the trees a ghostly white. She tiptoed out onto the porch, her breath sending frosty little clouds into the air.

"Squawk!"

The sound had come from the pen. Her knees suddenly went weak. Taking a deep breath to shore up her courage, she took one wobbly step into the backyard. And then another. She wanted desperately to stop. To turn around and run back into the house where she could jump into her bed and hide her head under the pillow. But she couldn't. She had to go on. She took another step, using the two glowing red eyes to guide her to the fence.

"Squuaawwk!"

She was standing face-to-beak with Frankenturkey. The big bird swelled up his chest like a balloon and glared at her. His eyes flamed even brighter.

But it was his breast that drew her attention. It gave off a deep-red glow. She could see the outline of the wishbone inside, pulsing like a flashing neon light.

If . . . if only I hadn't given it to him, she thought, choking back a sob. *The wishbone was what changed this creature from my beloved Gobble-de-gook into a monster.*

"Oh, Gobble-de-gook," Annie wailed. "I'm sorry. I'm *so* sorry I did this to you. I love you, Gobble-de-gook! I love you!"

"SQUUAAWWK!" screamed the monster turkey.

It staggered back a step and shook its head. The wishbone pulsed faster and brighter until Annie had to shade her eyes with a hand.

"You monster!" she cried. "It's all your fault! I'll get that wishbone back! I *will*! I swear I will, if it's the last thing I *ever* do!"

She opened the gate and marched into the pen.

Chapter

Frankenturkey spread his wings and lunged for Annie. She was suddenly engulfed in a heavy blanket of wings! Smothering her! Forcing her to the ground!

"Help!" she cried, struggling to get away. Her cry was muffled by the huge turkey's feathers.

His enormous body weighed down on her. He reared his head back and slashed at her with his razor-sharp beak.

She tried to shove him away.

"Oh, Gobble-de-gook," she said in a weak voice. "I know it's your body. Help me if you can—*please help me!*"

Frankenturkey froze in midair. His eyes blazed fiendishly.

"AAAAWWWWKKKK!"

He staggered backward and shook his head.

"AAAWWWKKK! AAAWWWKKK! AAAWWWKKK!" Regaining his balance, the monster lunged forward again, his swordlike beak slashing out at her.

Annie rolled to one side a split second before his beak tore into the ground beside her head.

The giant bird's breast was swelling even more, and the wishbone was pulsing harder and harder.

"GOBBLE-DE-GOOK! PLEASE HELP ME!" she screamed.

Again, Frankenturkey staggered backward. He teetered for a moment and fell, landing in a mountain of feathers in the corner of the pen.

"AAWW—AAWW—" he choked. "EEERRRGGG!"

Annie watched in terror as the huge bird made another gigantic try to get to his feet, but something seemed to be pulling him back.

Again he struggled to get up. Again he fell back. Forward and backward he went as he strained to get at her.

Annie gasped. "Oh, Gobble-de-gook! It's you! Finally! I know it is. I love you!" she whispered.

As if in answer, the glow in Frankenturkey's chest swelled—growing and spreading until it lit up the night sky. Suddenly a red ball appeared between the forks of the wishbone, bending and pushing them apart.

Annie stared in disbelief. It wasn't a ball! It was the shape of a heart! It was pulsing and pushing the forks of the wishbone farther and farther apart!

There was a loud "SNAP!" as the wishbone broke in two.

At that instant, the giant heart burst out of the bird's chest, spewing a tidal wave of blood over Frankenturkey's startled face.

He raised his head, giving one last gigantic "SQUUUAAAWWWK!" before sinking to the ground. His wings fluttered weakly. The fiery eyes flickered and faded like a pair of dying embers.

Annie thought her own heart would burst. She fell to her knees, stroking Gobble-de-gook's lifeless head.

"Oh, Gobble-de-gook," she sobbed. "You did this for me. I brought you back to life. And now you've given your own new life to save all of us from Frankenturkey!"

As if to reply, the big bird let out one last sigh, and the two halves of the wishbone slid across the snow, stopping beside Annie.

"Oh, thank you, Gobble-de-gook. I love you," she whispered.

The nightmare was over. Annie put her face in her hands and cried softly. Now she understood why she had been the only one not under Frankenturkey's spell.

It was because of Gobble-de-gook. Their love for each other had been like a shield, protecting her from the full fury of the monster's power. Her beloved pet hadn't been able to find his own power until the end when he was the only one who could save her. But he had done it, and she was safe.

Suddenly the lights flashed on in her parents' bedroom. Then in Kyle's. Annie held her breath as the door flew open and her family poured out into the backyard.

"What's going on out here?" her father shouted.

"Annie, are you all right?" her mother cried. "We heard a terrible noise out here—" Mrs. Duggan froze in her tracks.

"Oh, no!" cried Kyle. "It's Gobble-de-gook! He's dead!"

Mr. Duggan rushed forward. "A wild animal must have broken into the pen and killed our turkey!" He glanced toward the woods, a concerned look spreading over his face.

"Uh-oh, there goes our Thanksgiving dinner," Kyle said.

"That's okay," Mrs. Duggan said. "We can always get another turkey." She put a loving arm around Annie. "The most important thing is that Annie's okay."

The sadness in Annie's heart melted away and was replaced by pure joy. There was no question about it now. Frankenturkey was gone. The wishbone no longer had any power.

The wishbone! Annie blinked and looked down at the ground. It had been lying there beside her a moment ago. Now it was gone!

Fear gripped her heart. *Where was it*? Had she only thought that Frankenturkey was gone?

"Brrrr. It's cold out here," said her father, blowing warm breath into his hands and stomping his feet on the snow-covered ground. "Let's go inside. We'll take care of this mess in the morning."

"But—" Annie started to protest as the panic inside her grew. She stopped and caught her breath. Then she burst out laughing.

Trouble was lying on the back porch, gnawing contentedly on two halves of a fork-shaped bone.

Look for

BONE CHILLERS

the TV series on ABC, Saturdays at 10:30 A.M., Eastern time. Check your local listings . . .

and prepare to be
SCARED!